PUBLISHING

ISBN : 978-1-893951-55-6

10 9 8 7 6 5 4 3 2

Design: Dynamo Limited
Text: Dynamo Limited
Interior Artwork: Ailin Chambers

For information regarding permission,
write to VP Intellectual Property, Ripley Entertainment Inc.,
Suite 188, 7576 Kingspointe Parkway, Orlando, Florida 32819

Email: publishing@ripleys.com
www.ripleysrbi.com

Manufactured in Dallas, PA, United States
in May/2010 by Offset Paperback Manufacturers

2nd printing

Collector card picture credits: t/l ©Megan Lorenz/fotolia.com

RUNNING WILD

PUBLISHING

a Jim Pattison Company

INTRODUCING THE RBI

Hidden away on a small island off the East Coast of the United States is Ripley High —a unique school for children who possess extraordinary talents.

Located in the former home of Robert Ripley—creator of the world-famous Ripley's Believe It or Not!—the school takes students who all share a secret. Although they look like you or me, they have amazing skills: the ability to conduct electricity, superhuman strength, or control over the weather— these are just a few of the talents the Ripley High School students possess.

The very best of these talented kids have been invited to join a top secret agency—Ripley's Bureau of Investigation: the RBI. This elite group operates from a hi-tech underground base hidden deep beneath the school. From here, the talented teen agents are sent on dangerous missions around the world, investigating sightings of fantastical creatures and strange occurrences. Join them on their incredible adventures as they seek out the weird and the wonderful, and try to separate fact from fiction ...

▶▶ RIPLEY

The Department of Unbelievable Lies

A mysterious rival agency determined to stop the RBI and discredit Ripley's by sabotaging the Ripley's database

The spirit of Robert Ripley lives on in RIPLEY, a supercomputer that stores the database—all Ripley's bizarre collections, and information on all the artifacts and amazing discoveries made by the RBI. Featuring a fully interactive holographic Ripley as its interface, RIPLEY gives the agents info on their missions and sends them invaluable data on their R-phones.

THE TEACHERS

▶▶ Mr. Cain

The agents' favorite teacher, Mr. Cain, runs the RBI—under the guise of a Museum Club— and coordinates all the agents' missions.

▶▶ Dr. Maxwell

The only other teacher at the school who knows about the RBI. Dr. Maxwell equips the agents for their missions with cutting-edge gadgets from his lab.

MEET THE RBI TEAM

As well as having amazing talents, each of the seven members of the RBI has expert knowledge in their own individual fields of interest. All with different skills, the team supports each other at school and while out on missions, where the three most suitable agents are chosen for each case.

The RBI team keep in touch with each other, while on missions, using their R-phones. They also receive facts and useful information from RIPLEY in this way.

▶▶ KOBE

NAME : Kobe Shakur

AGE : 15

SKILLS : Excellent tracking and endurance skills. tribal knowledge and telepathic abilities

NOTES : Kobe's parents grew up in different African tribes. Kobe has amazing tracking capabilities and is an expert on native cultures across the world. He can also tell the entire history of a person or object just by touching it.

▶▶ ZIA

NAME : Zia Mendoza

AGE : 13

SKILLS : Possesses magnetic and electrical powers. Can predict the weather

NOTES : The only survivor of a tropical storm that destroyed her village when she was a baby. Zia doesn't yet fully understand her abilities but she can predict and sometimes control the weather. Her presence can also affect electrical equipment.

▶▶ MAX

NAME : Max Johnson

AGE : 14

SKILLS : Computer genius and inventor

NOTES : Max, from Las Vegas, loves computer games and anything electrical. He spends most of his spare time inventing robots. Max hates school but he loves spending time helping Dr. Maxwell come up with new gadgets.

▶▶ KATE

▶▶ ALEK

NAME : Kate Jones

AGE : 14

SKILLS : Computer-like memory, extremely clever, and ability to master languages in minutes

NOTES : Raised at Oxford University in England, by her history professor and part-time archaeologist uncle, Kate memorized every book in the University library after reading them only once!

NAME : Alek Filipov

AGE : 15

SKILL : Contortionist with amazing physical strength

NOTES : Alek is a member of the Russian under-16 Olympic gymnastics team and loves sports and competitions. He is much bigger than the other agents, and although he seems quiet and serious much of the time, he has a wicked sense of humor.

▶▶ LI

NAME : Li Yong

AGE : 15

SKILL : Musical genius with pitch-perfect hearing and the ability to mimic any sound

NOTES : Li grew up in a wealthy family in Beijing, China, and joined Ripley High later than the other RBI agents. She has a highly developed sense of hearing and can imitate any sound she hears.

▶▶ JACK

NAME : Jack Stevens

AGE : 14

SKILLS : Can "talk" to animals and has expert survival skills

NOTES : Jack grew up on an animal park in the Australian outback. He has always shared a strong bond with animals and can communicate with any creature— and loves to eat weird food!

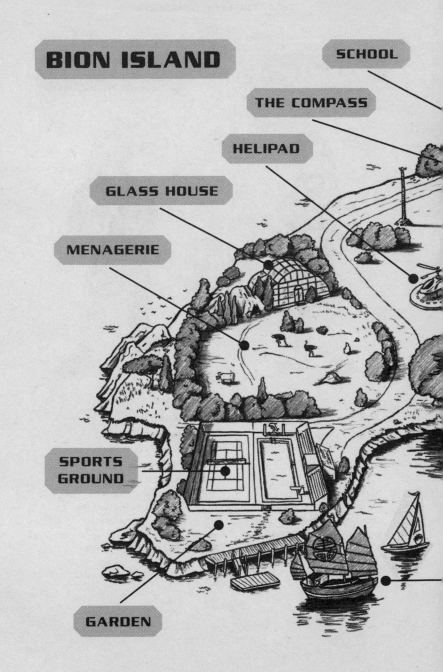

BION ISLAND

SCHOOL

THE COMPASS

HELIPAD

GLASS HOUSE

MENAGERIE

SPORTS GROUND

GARDEN

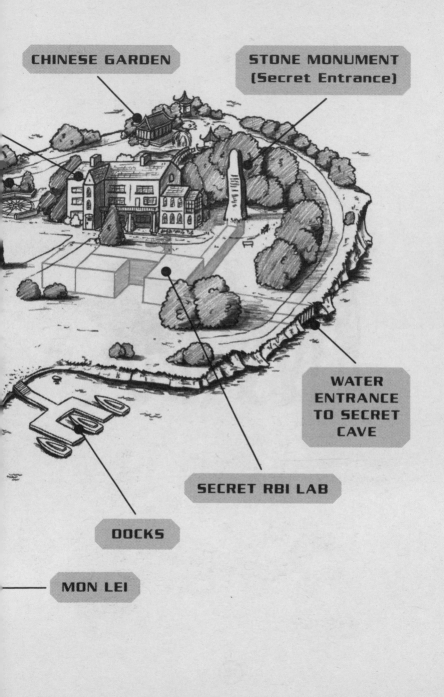

CHINESE GARDEN

STONE MONUMENT
[Secret Entrance]

WATER
ENTRANCE
TO SECRET
CAVE

SECRET RBI LAB

DOCKS

MON LEI

Prologue

10 years ago, somewhere over the border of western China.

The small plane buzzed like an angry hornet as it wheeled around beneath the clouds searching for somewhere to land, a plume of white smoke streaming from one engine. Clearly, it was in trouble ...

Suddenly, the plane banked sharply to the

left, heading for a small clearing in the vast expanse of forest below. As it came in to land it was losing height fast. Too fast! Its wings clipped the tops of the giant conifers, crashing through their upper branches. Nose-first, it plowed through the understory toward the clearing. The ground shook as the fuselage slammed down on the forest floor and shot like a giant missile toward a narrow gap in the trees, gouging a deep scar in the earth. With a sickening crunch, the nose crumpled as it was forced between two trees, the wings shearing off on impact. At last, the plane stopped.

The silence that followed was deafening. Time passed, but it was impossible to say how long. Then as the light began to fade, from somewhere inside the wreckage came the thin wail of a young child. It was a little girl, no more than five or six years old. Partly buried beneath luggage bags, she cried out for help, but no one came.

Barely conscious, the little girl struggled to free herself. Crawling on all fours, she made her way toward a gaping hole in the side of the fuselage and looked out. Then she struggled to her feet, climbed out from the plane, and stumbled into the darkening forest ...

Robo Snoop

"Where's Max?" asked Kate, looking up and down the empty corridor. "The R-phone message told us to go to the Museum Club right away."

"No idea," replied Jack, checking the message on his own R-phone. "The last I saw of him, he was sneaking around with one of his computerized creations. He's developed this wicked little gizmo with a hidden camera

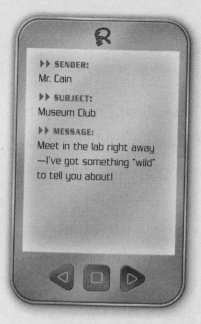

SENDER:
Mr. Cain

SUBJECT:
Museum Club

MESSAGE:
Meet in the lab right away
—I've got something "wild"
to tell you about!

that can see around corners. It can take digital images remotely, too. It's almost as if it is alive."

"Cool!" exclaimed Alek, who loved Max's creations. "What's he going to do with it?"

Jack shrugged. "Make trouble, I guess. He said he was planning a little 'private surveillance', whatever that means."

Kate frowned. Though one of the youngest members of the RBI team, she was also one of the most mature, and she couldn't bear Max's disregard for authority and the rules. In her mind, it was just plain irresponsible. The RBI agents had received an urgent Museum Club message and everyone had turned up—everyone except Max, that is. Obviously, he was too busy messing about with his electronic gadgets—or "toys" as Kate preferred to call them.

"What is it with Max?" she asked. "It's almost as if he wants to get in trouble. I wouldn't mind, but it puts all of us in danger when he does these things."

Though Jack got on well with Max and admired his free spirit, he had to admit Kate had a point. She usually did. All the agents knew the Ripley Bureau of Investigation was top secret,

and Mr. Cain had drummed into them the vital importance of being discreet. Max's constant mischief and kicking against authority could only lead to trouble ...

"It's pointless wasting energy getting angry," said Kobe calmly. "Let's just concentrate on finding Max. He's got to be around here somewhere."

"If anyone can find him, Li can," said Zia confidently. The others nodded, and looked expectantly at Li. Her amazing supersensitive

hearing skills were legendary at Ripley High, even though she had only been there for two years.

"It's good to know you have such confidence in me," said Li with a laugh. "In fact, I already know where he is."

"Wow! That was quick work!" exclaimed Kate, totally impressed by her friend's unique gift.

Li, who was standing outside Mr. Willis's office, grinned. "Actually, I didn't really have to use my abilities," she admitted. "He wasn't that hard to find." She beckoned the others over.

Kate, Jack, Alek, and the others crowded around the door. Inside, Max, Mr. Willis, and a very cross Mr. Clarkson could clearly be heard, having a heated "discussion" about Max's latest escapade.

"You might call it 'Robo Snoop', Mr. Johnson," snapped the furious teacher. "I call it spying. Mr. Clarkson was extremely upset at the invasion of his privacy."

Jack grinned in spite of himself. Mr. Clarkson was the school caretaker, and he was always snooping on the pupils of Ripley High.

"It's about time someone gave him a taste of his own medicine," he chuckled.

"Shh!" whispered Zia, leaning in closer.

"You—" Mr. Clarkson began, but Mr. Willis was on a roll.

"You can take that smirk off your face—along with those ridiculous sunglasses," he continued. "Your behavior is nothing to smile about, believe me. And neither are your school grades. They are a disgrace for a young man of your abilities. It's about time you improved your attitude and put in some hard work for a change. Your last essay for me on Mutating Minerals was sketchy, to say the least."

"Sorry, Sir," replied Max, not sounding in the least bit apologetic, and trying not to laugh. Mr. Willis had rather large ears, which stuck out at the side of his head, and whenever the teacher got cross those ears flushed bright red. Right now they were dark pink, a sign that Mr. Willis was on his way to being quite furious. "I was away on a field trip," Max continued. "I didn't have much time to finish it—fascinating though Mutating Minerals are, of course."

"And that brings me to my next point," boomed Mr. Willis, ignoring the sarcasm in Max's voice. "How can you possibly keep up with your work when you are constantly going away on field trips? You missed an entire module from the Artifact Studies syllabus last term. It really is most irregular. What on earth can you be doing on all these trips? Are they really necessary?"

The others could sense Max's discomfort at this line of questioning, even through the closed door. Going on "field trips" was the RBI cover story for their special missions. Mr. Willis's questions were getting dangerously close to the mark.

"You'd better ask Mr. Cain about that, Sir," replied Max, sounding slightly less cocky for once.

"What precisely was the nature of your last field trip?" asked Mr. Willis, sensing Max's discomfort, too. "Perhaps you would care to enlighten me?"

"Uh-oh!" murmured Kate, looking alarmed. "I don't like the way this conversation is going."

Wolf Boy

On the other side of the door, Max was experiencing an unfamiliar sensation—rising panic. In spite of his bravado, he knew that one wrong word about the "field trips" could put the whole of the RBI team and their missions in jeopardy. And Mr. Willis was like a dog with a bone—there was no way he was going to let go of the subject now ...

"Come on, Mr. Johnson," barked Mr. Willis,

enjoying the fact that he had the upper hand. "I'm waiting."

The others listened anxiously, ears pressed to the door.

"We've got to do something," whispered Kobe, picking up Max's vibes. "He isn't going to talk his way out of this one easily ..."

Alex nodded. "We need to distract Mr. Willis—and we need to do it right now." He raised his hand to knock.

"Stop!" hissed Li. "Interrupting Mr. Willis will only make him more mad, and you'll both end up in trouble."

The others had to agree. It was no use making the situation any worse.

"Send Kate in," suggested Alek suddenly. "Mr. Willis won't get angry with her."

The others looked at each other. Kate was Mr. Willis's star pupil. Her enthusiasm and knowledge in his lessons never ceased to impress and delight the fussy teacher. Alek was right. Kate was definitely the man—or rather girl—for the mission.

Reluctant though she felt, Kate agreed. "The things I do for you lot," she smiled grimly. "Wish me luck!" She knocked loudly on the door.

"Come in, if you must," snapped Mr. Willis's impatient voice, sounding less than pleased. "Ah! Miss Jones," he continued, his voice softening just a fraction as Kate peered around the door. "I'm rather busy at the moment. Can it wait?"

"I'm sorry to interrupt, Mr. Willis," said Kate, the model of politeness. "I didn't know you had anyone in here. It's about your latest homework assignment. I don't think I'm on track for an "A", and I was hoping you could give me some further reading. Shall I come back?"

Mr. Willis hesitated. There was nothing he liked more than to talk about his subject, especially when the listener was so appreciative.

"No, no, come in," he smiled. "Mr. Johnson and I can continue our conversation a little later—in detention."

Relieved, Max made a quick exit, turning only to wink at Kate as he left the room. Needless to say, Kate did not return the gesture.

"G'day, mate," said Jack, slapping Max on the shoulder as he appeared in the corridor. "That was close."

Max waited for Mr. Clarkson, who had also left Mr. Willis's room, to walk out of sight before he grinned at the others. "You saved my life, team! I thought he'd never let up ..."

Just then the door opened and Kate came out.

"Thanks again, Mr. Willis," she said over her shoulder. "I'll go to the library right away. That book sounds fascinating."

The agents set off down the corridor. Max, who always delighted in winding up Kate, sneaked up behind her.

"That book sounds fascinating!" he mimicked, doing a poor imitation of her English accent.

Kate, however, wasn't in the mood for games. "If it wasn't for me you'd still be in there, Mr. oh-so-cool," she snapped. "So do me a favor and keep your stupid comments to yourself."

"No sweat!" laughed Max. "I had everything under control anyway."

Kate snorted. "Why can you never admit when you are wrong!" she said. "You could have put the whole team in danger."

Max flushed, and Kate saw her comment had hit home. If only he would stop and think.

Keen to stop the bickering, Alek held up his hands. "I'm declaring a truce!" he announced. "Now can we just get going before Mr. Cain thinks we've all left the building?"

The seven agents headed down the corridor that was filled with strange artifacts that Robert Ripley had collected on his worldwide travels. Finally they stopped in front of the statue, or the head of one anyway. Liu Min, the double-pupil man, stared back at them from his wooden panel. The head also contained a hidden eye-recognition scanner that granted access to the secret RBI base. Max scanned the corridor. "All clear," he declared. "Alek, why don't you do the honors?"

Alek stepped forward, lining his right eye up with the scanner, Liu Min's left double pupil, and almost at once the whole panel

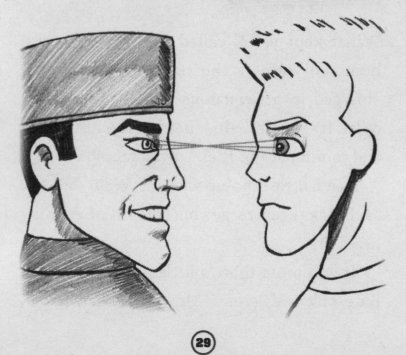

▶▶ Liu Ch'ung, or Liu Min, as he was sometimes known, was born with double pupils in each eye. Despite this, he became a powerful soldier and politician in China in the 10th century. Double pupils were often associated with a supernatural "evil eye" curse, but are actually caused by birth defects in the eye that appear to be extra pupils.

on which the statue was mounted swung forward, revealing a doorway and a twisting staircase leading down into the basement of the old school-house, and to the RBI base ...

"What kept you?" called a firm but good-humored voice as the seven agents finally emerged in a cavernous but ultra-modern cellar. It was Mr. Cain—head of the RBI team and coordinator of their special missions.

"Just a little hold-up with Mr. Willis, Sir ..." said Max, keen to get his version of events heard first.

"It was more than 'a little hold-up'!" cried Kate, obviously cross. "Mr. Willis was digging for information on our field trips. He was trying to get Max to tell him all about them."

"It's almost as if he knows there's something more to them," said Li.

"Of course, Mr. Clarkson was there too," said Max, keen to keep everyone's focus on something other than what he had done wrong. "I'm sure there's something dodgy about him. He's always nosing around the RBI."

Mr. Cain listened as the team related the full story. "Don't worry, I'll keep an eye on the situation," he told the concerned agents when they had finished. "But I think it's unlikely to be anything to worry about. Now let's get to the reason I called you here. RIPLEY has information about some interesting sightings in the Hengduan Mountains on the border of western China."

At once, the agents fell silent and turned to face a desk in the corner. Hovering just above it like some weird ghostly apparition was the

floating head of Robert Ripley, founder of Ripley High, and recorder of all things unusual.

"Hello agents," said the head, smiling faintly. "Thank you for coming."

Max grinned in appreciation. "Nice to be here," he replied. Even now, after so many mission briefings, he was still in awe of the unique technology that made this conversation possible. Of course, the head wasn't real— it was a holographic link to an impressive artificial intelligence system—but sometimes it felt pretty real.

Once all the agents had greeted him, RIPLEY began to speak.

"Inhabitants of a small mountain village in the Hengduan region have reported sightings of a wolf pack coming into the village to scavenge for food," he began.

"I don't get it," said Jack, whose knowledge and understanding of the animal world was vast. "It's quite unusual for wolves to be that close to the Chinese border, but it's not really the kind of thing we investigate, is it?"

"There's more," said Mr. Cain. "There have been sightings of what could possibly be a teenage boy living among the wolves."

"But who is he?" asked Zia, intrigued. "Where did he come from?"

"We have been contacted by a local girl called Mya. She thinks he might be her brother, who disappeared in a plane crash ten years ago," continued RIPLEY. "Your mission is to find out if there is any truth behind these sightings of the wolf boy, and establish his identity, should he exist."

"Have I been selected for this mission?" asked Jack, struggling to keep the excitement out of his voice. Everything about this case had his name stamped on it.

"Of course," replied Mr. Cain. "Your expertise with animals will be essential for interacting with the wolves and the boy, especially if there's any trouble. Kobe will be going with you. His tracking abilities might be needed in the mountains and forests that surround the location."

Kobe nodded that he would be happy to go too.

"Can I be the third team member?" asked Max, keen to redeem himself after the afternoon's events.

Mr. Cain shook his head. "I want Kate to go," he explained. "Her language skills will be useful with the locals, and she might be able to help communicate with the boy if he doesn't speak in a language that we are familiar with."

Max looked disappointed.

"You only want to go to escape your detention with Mr. Willis," teased Li, trying to lift Max out of his mood.

"It was worth a try," grinned Max, rising to the challenge.

Mr. Cain laughed. "This is one detention I think Max is going to have to do."

Territory and Tracking

Immediately after the briefing, Kate, Kobe, and Jack began planning for their mission.

"Our flight to China leaves in less than 16 hours. That doesn't give us long to prepare," said Kate. "Shall I go to the library to research the area?"

"It would be quicker to go straight to Miss Burrows," Jack pointed out. "That will leave more time to study the reports of the crash and wolf boy sightings, and to make our plan of action."

The others agreed. Miss Burrows was their geography teacher, and a favorite with the team. Though she had no idea about the existence of the RBI and their missions, she often unknowingly helped them by providing information about the locations they traveled to.

The three agents made their way to Miss Burrows's office. Luckily, it was lunchtime and the young teacher was sitting at her desk, eating a sandwich.

"Hello," she smiled, brushing the crumbs from her sweater. "What can I do for you?"

Kate, Jack, and Kobe had a cover story ready.

"I'm planning a trip to China at the end of term," said Jack, "and maybe a visit to the Hengduan Mountain region on the western Chinese border. I've heard the wildlife there is amazing. I was hoping you could tell me a little more about the territory."

"Good choice!" exclaimed Miss Burrows, brimming with enthusiasm. "A remarkable area, though very remote in places. You would need to a charter a light aircraft to access much of the region."

Jack smiled to himself. You could always rely on Miss Burrows. Once started, it was difficult to stop her ...

Miss Burrows pulled out an enormous atlas from a shelf, leafed through the pages, and laid it out on her desk.

"The Hengduan Mountains are one of the only ranges in China to run north to south," she told them, pointing on the map.

"Doesn't the name Hengduan mean 'to transect'?" asked Kate, whose knowledge of languages was unrivaled at Ripley High.

"That's right," nodded Miss Burrows, unable to hide a smile at Kate's amazing memory.

"OK, show off!" smirked Jack. "Just because

you can speak every language under the sun ..."

"Not EVERY language," corrected Kate, grinning. "Just 14—fluently. I don't count all the others."

Jack pulled a face at Kate's correction. Sometimes she could be such a know-it-all.

Miss Burrows continued, ignoring their squabble. "The Hengduan range 'transects', or borders, China, dividing it from several other countries, including Myanmar in the south. The region you are planning to visit is really quite difficult to get to—which is what makes it so special. It's made up of a series of mountain ridges and deep river valleys. It's very tricky, but an extremely beautiful landscape."

"What about the plant life?" asked Kobe, fascinated by the picture Miss Burrows was painting.

"Thick conifer forests, mainly," replied Miss Burrows. "The area didn't completely freeze during the ice ages, so it's bursting with rare wildlife and plants! It's a zoologist's paradise! You'll love it, Jack."

▶▶ The Champawat man-eating tiger, who lived in Nepal and India about 100 years ago, was rumored to have killed 436 people.

▶▶ A hungry tiger can eat almost 110 pounds of meat in one meal—equivalent to a person consuming more than 400 quarter-pound burgers.

"Isn't it home to the giant panda?" asked Kate.

"That's right," nodded Miss Burrows, "and many other species too, including some very rare primates and deer—even tigers! How do you fancy a chat with a wild tiger?"

Jack laughed, though Miss Burrows wasn't actually joking. An ability to communicate with wild beasts was one of the abilities that had gotten Jack to Ripley High—though 'chat' was probably a slight exaggeration. "Wow! Now that sounds like my kind of trip!" he exclaimed, genuinely excited.

When they had finished, Miss Burrows showed them out with a smile. "If you do go, bring me back some photos," she told Jack. "I'm very envious!"

The agents made their way down the corridor without talking. Much as they longed to discuss everything that they had learned, they couldn't risk being overheard by other students.

"Where next?" asked Kobe, breaking into Kate's and Jack's thoughts. "A visit to Dr. Maxwell?"

Dr. Maxwell was in charge of the technology department at Ripley High, and the only other teacher in the whole school to know about the RBI. The ultimate techno wizard, he equipped the agents with everything they needed for their missions—and more.

Kate looked at her watch and nodded.

"Mr. Cain said he had arranged for us to find Dr. Maxwell in the technology lab just about now."

Sure enough, Dr. Maxwell was expecting them. "No Max today?" he asked. "Shame! I wanted to show him this new tracking software I've been working on. It would be the perfect 'app' for his new Snooping Bot, or whatever it is called."

"I think you mean Robo Snoop," laughed Jack.

"And I don't think Max needs any more applications for that particular creation," said Kate disapprovingly. "It's already got him into a lot of trouble, and he risked exposing the whole RBI. 'The Detention Finder' would have been a better name for it."

"Oh dear, poor Max," Dr. Maxwell chuckled. "Keeping out of trouble was never his strong point. My strong point, however, is most definitely gadgets ..."

He opened a drawer and placed a small, flat object on the table, no bigger than an MP3 player. "In addition to your standard kit, I've got a couple more gizmos for you. This is the very latest in advanced tracking systems. I've been developing the software in partnership with the Space Program. It links up to a series of satellites in space, so you can download continuous images of a traveling target's precise location on Earth, as it moves."

"Awesome!" said Kobe. "A bit like those cool online street maps."

"Exactly," said Dr. Maxwell. "But a bit more high-tech than those even. It makes use of the very latest in heat-sensing technology, so it can supply images even in the dark. There's just one small problem. The system is still in testing, and I'm concerned that the thick forest canopy where you are going may interfere with the satellite signal. It will be most interesting to see how it performs. On the bright side, if image contact is lost, the system will still relay standard Global Positioning System data to the receiver."

"No worries!" said Jack, clapping Kobe on the back. "Kobe's tracking skills are better than old-fashioned GPS, any day!"

Next, Dr. Maxwell handed Kate what looked like bracelets with a round metal pendant dangling from each one.

"These are the tracking devices that work with the system," he told her. "They emit a signal that is picked up by the satellites, revealing the travel activities of the subject, including the speed and direction of travel, time, and precise location. In addition to the continuous images, you can download all this information on the receiver."

▶▶ A stolen snake was found thanks to its meal—an endangered marsupial fitted with a tracking device. The 6 foot 7 inch python was taken by thieves from a research center just after it had eaten the creature. After picking up the signal from the air, scientists and police tracked it on foot to a house.

"We might be able to put one on the wolf boy to keep track of him in the forest," exclaimed Kate.

Kobe held out his hand to Dr. Maxwell. "Thank you, Sir," he said. "Your help will be invaluable, as always."

Dr. Maxwell smiled and shook Kobe's hand. "It's my pleasure, agent Shakur. And don't forget, I expect a full report on the success—or otherwise—of my gadgets when you return."

In the Hengduan Mountains

Twelve hours later, Kobe, Kate, and Jack were gazing out of a plane at the forested slopes below.

Kobe and Jack chatted, their faces pressed against the window as they searched for the narrow strip in the valley where their plane would land. Kate, on the other hand, was lost in thought as she replayed what RIPLEY had told them over and over in her mind. The girl,

Mya, was just five years old when she had lost her little brother in the plane crash. Would she be able to recognize him again after all this time? And if the wolf boy did turn out to be Mya's long lost brother, would he be able to recognize his sister after ten long years? It seemed unlikely. Kate had lost her own parents in a car accident just a few years ago, and even she struggled to recall their faces sometimes—despite her incredible memory powers.

"We're coming in to land," said Kobe, tapping Kate on the shoulder. "Ready for action, agent Jones?"

Kate nodded, banishing the difficult memories. "We're here to discover the truth," she told herself. "So let's get down to business."

A small group of locals greeted them at the landing strip to guide them up to the mountain village where Mya was waiting. Kate translated their welcome for Kobe and Jack.

"They say it's a long trek up to the village,"

she told the others. "We must leave at once."

It was already past midday, and the sun was high in the sky as they set off. The forest was dense, and only the occasional shaft of light broke through the trees. Even so, the agents soon found their backs dripping with sweat from the effort. Even with their high-altitude training at Ripley High, they were finding it difficult to breathe in the thin air.

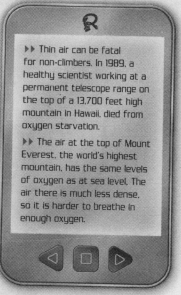

▶▶ Thin air can be fatal for non-climbers. In 1989, a healthy scientist working at a permanent telescope range on the top of a 13,700 feet high mountain in Hawaii, died from oxygen starvation.

▶▶ The air at the top of Mount Everest, the world's highest mountain, has the same levels of oxygen as at sea level. The air there is much less dense, so it is harder to breathe in enough oxygen.

"Whoah!" panted Jack, pausing for breath. "And I thought BION Island was hard to get to. This place is something else!"

Kobe nodded. "We must have passed the 10,000 feet mark by now," he replied, noticing changes in plant life. "It can't be much further."

But though it was hard work, the agents were all really pleased to be there. The air was fresh with the scent of spruce and exotic flowers, and all around, the forest called to them. Jack could hardly contain his excitement.

"Did you know this region is home to 237 species of mammals alone?" he asked, scanning the surrounding forest with his RBI standard-

issue binoculars.

Finally, after more than an hour of hiking, the vegetation began to thin out, and the agents arrived at their destination—a collection of wooden houses built around a central clearing. There to welcome them was a tall, slender girl about 15 years of age.

"Welcome," said the girl in perfect English.

"Thank you for coming."

"You must be Mya," said Kate, as she stepped forward to shake the girl's hand. "Your English is excellent."

Mya smiled. "I have studied hard," she said. "I hoped speaking English would help me to talk to visitors and hopefully find my brother. Please, come sit by the fire and eat. I must tell you my story."

Kate, Jack, and Kobe accepted gratefully. Though it was only mid-afternoon, there was already a chill in the air and they had not eaten for hours. They listened in silence as Mya began her tale.

"It was ten years ago," she told them quietly. My father was flying the plane. My mother and three-year-old brother Arun were with us. All I can remember is that one minute we were in the air, and the next I was crawling out of the wreckage of the plane. I was rescued by the locals when I wandered into their village."

"Did anyone ever go back to the site of the crash?" asked Kate gently, knowing it must be painful for Mya to talk about these things.

Mya nodded. "Some villagers went back to the site to help, but my parents were already dead. There was no sign of my little brother Arun. Some people said a tiger must have taken him, but I've always believed he is still out there."

"Tell us about the sightings," said Jack. "When did they begin?"

"The rumors began many years ago when the wolves first started coming to the village. People said there was a strange cub that looked almost human, but acted like a wolf. Only a few people have seen it, though many talk of it."

At this point, the leader of the village spoke up excitedly. Kate listened with interest, then quickly translated for the others.

"He says that some believe the cub is half human, half wolf, but others say it is a werewolf."

Jack frowned. "A werewolf? Now that really would be a first for the database. I checked with RIPLEY before we left. As far as the records are concerned, there's no concrete proof for the existence of such a creature, despite all the myths and legends."

"And what does he believe?" asked Kobe, looking at the village leader.

There was a quick exchange between Kate

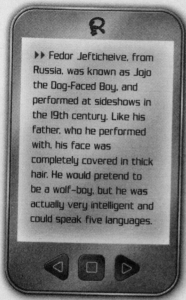

▶▶ Fedor Jefticheive, from Russia, was known as Jojo the Dog-Faced Boy, and performed at sideshows in the 19th century. Like his father, who he performed with, his face was completely covered in thick hair. He would pretend to be a wolf-boy, but he was actually very intelligent and could speak five languages.

and the man.

"He has seen the creature with his own eyes. He is sure it is a young boy, maybe 12 or 13 years old."

"That's the age that Arun would be now," cried Mya. "It has to be him! Don't you see?"

Moved by the emotion in her voice, Jack turned toward the girl.

"It won't be long before the light begins to fade and the wolves will come out to feed. Can you take us to the place where they appear?"

Mya nodded. "It's a small glade on the edge of the village."

"Let's put out some food for them," suggested Kobe. "It's highly unlikely the wolf boy will turn up, but we can take one of Dr. Maxwell's tracking devices off the bracelet and hide it in the food. If the wolves take the bait, we will be able to follow the pack and hopefully find the boy among them."

Everyone agreed.

Just before dusk, Jack placed the meat, with the small metallic tracking device hidden inside it, on the edge of the glade. Then he joined the others again, concealed in the bushes down-wind.

"Let's hope they're not fussy eaters," murmured Kobe, as Jack crouched down.

"Sshh!" whispered Jack. "I think we're about to find out!"

The sound of howling echoed through the forest, signaling the approach of the wolf pack. The agents and Mya held their breath as the undergrowth stirred, and one large male, followed by a female and her young, stepped out into the open.

The magnificent male sniffed the air. Calmly, he padded across the clearing toward the food, accompanied by excited yips and low growls from the rest of the pack. It was feeding time. Snatching the meat in his awesome jaws, he began to feast noisily. Moments later, the female joined in, tearing at the meat with relish. At last it was the turn of the young wolves. Snarling

and biting at each other, they squabbled over the leftovers.

"Game on," Jack mouthed to Kobe and Kate. "They've taken the bait!"

The agents shivered as an eerie howl echoed across the glade. It was coming from the forest nearby. The male and female wolf turned expectantly, showing no fear. Suddenly, a creature the size of a large dog crashed through the undergrowth, and broke through into the clearing. It looked around, taking in its surroundings and sniffing out the food. Standing up on its hind legs, it gave a loud bark, and pushed its straggling hair back to reveal a human face. It was the wolf boy!

Talking with Wolves

"ARUN!" shouted Mya, her cry cutting through the cold air. At the sound of her voice, the wolves froze for an instant, before turning tail and disappearing into the forest. Only the wolf boy remained, with his head cocked to one side as if somehow puzzled.

Unable to hold herself back, Mya struggled to crawl out of her hiding place.

"It's my brother!" she cried. "I know it is!"

"No, Mya!" whispered Jack, grabbing hold of her arm. "You'll startle him."

But it was too late. The noise had spooked the wolf boy. With one last look over his shoulder, he leaped effortlessly over a log and vanished into the undergrowth to join the pack.

"Come back!" called Mya, breaking free of Jack's hold and chasing after the boy. "It's me, Mya!"

Mya disappeared into the forest, with Kobe, Jack and Kate hot on her tail.

"This way!" called Kobe, picking up the scent of the wolves at once. "Follow me!"

Kate thrust the receiver for Dr. Maxwell's tracking system into his hand as she caught up. "You'd better take this," she panted. "It's working. Look!"

"Thank you, Dr. Maxwell!" grinned Kobe, studying the incredibly clear image and data on the screen. "The pack is heading east for the gorge. We've got them! Let's go, guys!"

Up ahead, a large rock face loomed starkly out of the forest. They were entering river valley country.

"Watch your footing," warned Kobe. "The landscape here can change suddenly. According to this little gadget, we're skirting the edge of a very deep river valley. It would be easy to slip and fall ..."

As they ran, the forest rang with an ear-splitting series of whistles and shrieks.

"Did you see that?" panted Jack, as a flash of gold streaked past them overhead. "That was a snub-nosed monkey. This place is amazing. What I wouldn't give to get a closer look at the wildlife ..."

"How about that for a closer look?" hissed Kate, stopping dead in her tracks. Blocking their way was a fully-grown male wolf. The beast lowered its head, ears pulled flat and its upper lip curled to expose a vicious set of teeth.

"Back off slowly," Jack hissed, taking control

at once. "And don't make eye contact. That's one unhappy wolf ..."

Hardly daring to breathe, the group retreated back up the track.

"What now?" asked Mya, when they finally

felt safe enough to stop. "We can't lose the trail. We've come so far!"

"Don't worry," Jack reassured her. "We've got a secret weapon—Kobe! Tracking is his thing. He's amazing at it."

Kobe smiled modestly, and checked the screen. "It looks like the wolf pack is resting about a mile from here, by some caves. All we need to do now is find a different route."

He knelt down to examine the ground and lower branches of the surrounding vegetation. "This way!" he said, pointing at a narrow path hidden by the undergrowth. "The wolves use a number of tracks in this area, but this one has been used very recently—within the last 15 minutes, I'd say."

Kobe's confidence was short-lived. After just a few minutes of walking, the team found their way blocked yet again—this time by a sleek female, snarling aggressively. Kobe changed direction again, then again, but it was no use—

each time the wolves barred their way.

"Clever devils," whistled Jack admiringly. "They're cutting us off."

He was right. Little by little, the wolf pack closed in on them until finally the agents realized that they were completely surrounded.

"Any ideas gratefully received," breathed Kate, her arm protectively around Mya, shielding her from the wolves.

"I think it's time for a little wolf talk,"

whispered Kobe. "Jack, can you use your ability to calm them?"

"I can try," replied Jack. "But these animals are angry ... very angry."

Moving slowly, he knelt down on all fours, keeping his body as low to the floor as he could. Avoiding eye contact, he approached the largest male in the pack, making low, whispering noises and singing softly.

The others watched in awe as Jack's deep

link with animals began to work its magic, somehow calming and soothing the beast.

"It's working!" murmured Kate, as the wolf's aggressive body language began to change.

Suddenly, one female wolf barked sharply. At once, the male began to snap and snarl at Jack, its body resuming a highly aggressive pose.

Jack backed off immediately.

"It's no use," he told the others. "It's not working. They see us as a threat to Arun—he's one of their own."

As he spoke, the wolves began to advance, closing a tighter and tighter circle around them ...

Coming Home

"Listen!" cried Kate. "What's that?"

A lone wolf was barking in the forest somewhere nearby.

The pack responded noisily, all barking, yipping, and howling together. Moments later, the bushes parted and the wolf boy launched himself into the fray, landing between the wolves and the agents.

"It's Arun!" cried Mya.

The agents watched in amazement as the largest female in the pack approached the boy, ears forward and tail wagging.

"Incredible!" murmured Jack under his breath. The she-wolf was licking the boy, and nuzzling his cheek, as the wolf boy whined like a pup. "It's almost as if he's her own baby."

Seizing the chance, Mya crouched down and

crawled forward. Slowly, she inched toward the wolf boy, copying the low body position that Jack had adopted earlier. At once, the wolves began to snarl and growl.

"Come back!" called Kate. "It's too dangerous."

Mya refused to listen. "I have to do this," she said. Very slowly, she lifted her head and looked into the boy's eyes.

"Arun," she said softly. "Do you remember me? I'm your sister."

The boy gave no sign of understanding, but neither did he move away. Instead, he gazed back at Mya as if trying to remember something.

The female wolf snarled angrily.

"This is crazy!" cried Kate. "Jack, stop her!"

But Jack shook his head. "Something's happening. Look!"

As he spoke, the wolf boy gave a low bark. At once, the female began to back off. The other wolves were retreating, too. One by one they melted into the forest.

The wolf boy and Mya now faced each other, motionless.

"What now?" whispered Kobe. "How do we communicate with him?"

Kate stepped forward. "Listen to me, Mya," she said. "It's clear this boy feels a connection with you. Otherwise he would have run away by now. We need to build on that, and tell him who you are in a language he understands."

"But he doesn't understand me!" said Mya. "It's obvious!"

"He does understand wolf language though," said Jack, suddenly catching on to Kate's line of reasoning. "You need to tell him in 'wolf' that you are family. Family relationships within a wolf pack are extremely strong. He needs to know you belong together."

"OK," said Mya slowly. "There's just one problem. I don't speak 'wolf'."

"But I know a girl who does," said Jack. "Kate!"

Mya looked unconvinced.

"I know it sounds weird," Kate explained, "but I have this strange skill. I only need to hear a language once and I can pick up the basics. It's a gift I was born with. I've only ever tried it with human languages before, but I've been listening to the noises the wolves make, and there seems to be a sort of pattern. I think I can help you 'talk' to him. Will you give it a try?"

▶▶ Washoe, a chimp born in West Africa, was taught 250 American Sign Language expressions. She passed on some of her knowledge to her adopted son Loulis.

▶▶ In 2008 a seven-year-old boy who spoke only in chirps was discovered in an apartment filled with birdcages. When he could not communicate with his rescuers, he flapped his arms like a bird.

"I'll try anything— as long as it gets my brother back," replied Mya. "Tell me what to do."

Kate took a deep breath. "Did you hear those funny growling noises the female made when she greeted the wolf boy?" she asked, mimicking the sounds perfectly to demonstrate. "You need to try and reproduce these noises as you approach him."

"Body language and smell are very important, too," added Jack. "Did you notice how the female nuzzled his face and touched him? They use smell to help identify members of the same family group."

Mya nodded. Feeling slightly foolish, she started to make the unfamiliar growling noises in the back of her throat, quietly to begin with, then louder as she grew in confidence. At first, the wolf boy just stared at Mya, but then he whined softly as if in reply.

"He's talking to you," whispered Kate, encouragingly. "Keep going."

Very gradually the wolf boy moved closer, sniffing Mya's hair, until she could almost touch him. Slowly, she reached out and placed her hand on his cheek, still making the strange sounds. The wolf boy whimpered, as a look of understanding finally dawned on his face. Never taking his eyes of hers, he reached out to touch her too …

"My brother!" murmured Mya, pulling him in her arms and sinking to the ground, where they stayed, curled up together.

The others came over. Very gently, Kobe placed his hand on the wolf boy's arm. He sighed deeply as his unique ability allowed him to connect with the child, sharing his memories and feelings.

"There's a plane crash," he said to Mya at last, "and a sense of loss—great loss! There's no doubt in my mind. This boy is Arun."

"We all want him to be Arun," said Kate, always skeptical of Kobe's more mystical abilities. "But there's one way to be sure."

She opened her rucksack and pulled out a mini fingerprint scanner and DNA sampling set—standard issue for all RBI agents.

"I'll send this back to base for identity

confirmation," she told Mya, taking a quick scan of the boy's finger and gently wiping his mouth with a cotton swab. Arun snarled and tried to back away from Kate, but Mya held him firmly and tried to reassure him. "It's the only way you can be certain," Kate told her, running another cotton swab around the inside of Mya's cheek. "This will give us something to compare the first sample to," she explained. "They will be able to look for DNA markers at the lab that tell them if the two of you are related."

Mya nodded and then held out her hand to the wolf boy. "It's time to go home," she told him. Silently, the boy took her hand. He gazed at it in wonder, then placed his own dirt-encrusted palm over the top of hers, comparing them. What he saw seemed to please him, and he yipped excitedly.

"Hand," said Mya in her native tongue— the language that Arun had spoken before the accident. She was encouraged by his response

and keen to make more progress with her lost brother. "Say HAND, Arun," she encouraged.

But the wolf boy just yipped and barked. He scampered around the circle of agents, touching their hands, faces, and hair, barking crazily.

"What's wrong? Why doesn't he speak?" asked Mya, troubled by his wild behavior.

"When he was little, he talked all the time."

"Ten years is a long time to live without language," replied Kate. "But don't worry. If he has already learned the rudimentary skills for the spoken language when he was a baby, he will almost certainly learn to speak again— though it may take some time."

"I hate to interrupt the fun," said Kobe, surveying the darkening forest. "But it's time we got back to the village. Night is falling, and we have a long way to go."

Mya nodded. "The forest is no place to be at night," she said. "Let's go."

When the agents arrived back at the village, news of their success spread quickly. Soon a large crowd of locals had gathered, eager to see the wolf child for themselves.

"Maybe we should warn everyone to back off," Kobe said to Kate. "We don't want to spook him."

But he worried needlessly. The wolf boy seemed unafraid. With Mya by his side, he sniffed around the village, exploring every nook and cranny, while the villagers observed him curiously.

"It looks like he's going to adapt to village life quite easily," said Jack, watching with amusement.

Kate laughed. "I think you're probably right, but I still asked Mya to put a tracking bracelet round Arun's ankle, just in case he feels the pull of the wild ..."

"So it's Arun now, is it?" teased Kobe, interrupting their conversation. "You weren't so sure earlier."

Kate grinned sheepishly. "I've just had the results back from base," she admitted. "There was a close genetic match. You were right. He is Mya's brother!"

"Tell me something I don't know," laughed Kobe.

Just then, Mya came up, a worried look on her face.

"It's time I settled Arun down for the night," she said. "It's been a very long day, and he's getting a little jumpy."

"I think I know why," said Jack. "Listen!"

Kate, Mya, and Kobe fell silent. The wolves in the forest were howling mournfully.

"They're calling to Arun," Jack explained. "He's still one of them, you know, and they think that he's lost."

"But he's not lost," cried Mya. "He's been found. For the first time in ten years, he's home."

"I don't think the wolves see it that way," said Jack.

"Look!" exclaimed Kate, looking at Arun. "What's he doing?"

Arun had climbed up on to the top of a woodpile, and was staring intently toward the forest. Suddenly, a chilling howl echoed

through the night air, sending a shiver down everyone's spine. Arun threw back his head and howled in reply. Turning to Mya and the agents, he barked sharply. Then, with a mighty leap, he sprang from the woodpile and ran off into the night ...

Tiger Attack

"No! Arun!" shouted Mya. "Come back! Don't leave me!" She turned to the others. "What did I do wrong?"

Kate put her arm around the distraught girl. "You didn't do anything wrong. The other wolves were calling him, and he had to go. As Jack says, he's one of their own."

"But he belongs to me, too," said Mya. "Doesn't that mean anything?"

"Of course it does," said Kate. "Anyone can see that he has a connection with you. In fact, I think Arun was trying to tell you something. I'm pretty certain that a sharp bark like that indicates danger or a threat of some kind. I believe he was trying to warn you ..."

"Maybe he was asking for help," suggested Jack. "Perhaps his pack is in danger."

"If Arun is in danger I must help him," said Mya, her voice charged with emotion. "Now that I have found him, I am not going to lose him again. I'm sorry," she cried, shaking off Kate's arm and starting to run in the direction Arun had gone. "I can't wait. I'm going after him."

The three agents watched helplessly as Mya disappeared into the darkness.

"We've got to find her," said Kate. "She's not thinking straight. Anything could happen to her out there in the forest. The wolves might find her before she finds Arun."

Pausing only to grab their tracking systems, the three agents set off in pursuit.

"She can't be far away," figured Jack, as they entered the forest. "It's Arun I'm most worried about. Let's check the tracking system. At least we can follow him on the screen this time."

"It might not be that easy!" called Kate. "Take a look."

Jack glanced at the screen. The image had disappeared. "The satellite must have lost the signal," he said. "Dr. Maxwell did warn us."

"He also said the receiver would still download basic GPS data," remembered Kate. "Let's try that."

Jack quickly opened a new window on the screen and activated the GPS application. Sure enough, a map with two moving red dots appeared on the screen, along with a host of other data.

"That's just brilliant!" declared Jack sarcastically. "How can we tell which dot is

Arun, and which is the wolf that ate the tracking device? I bet Max would know. Where is he when you need him?"

"Probably eating pizza and playing with his toys," quipped Kate, secretly agreeing with Jack that they could do with Max's help right about now, although she'd never let the boys know she felt that way!

Kobe thought for a moment. "We'll have to split up," he decided. "It's the only way that we can follow both targets. Jack, you take the first dot; Kate and I will take the second. We can stay in close communication via our radio-mic headsets while keeping a look out for Mya."

"I'll report back every five minutes," said Jack, as the three agents parted. "Unless something gets me, of course. Then, you'll probably hear my screams anyway!"

"Not funny, Jack," said Kate, grinning in spite of herself. "Just keep out of trouble, will you?"

Unfortunately, Kate and Kobe didn't have to go far before trouble found them. Almost immediately, they heard the sound of something, or someone, running through the forest. Mya stumbled out of the bushes, waving her arms wildly.

"RUN!" she wheezed, barely able to speak. "Tiger!"

For a moment, Kobe and Kate froze. This can't be happening, Kate thought to herself. But it was. Out of the darkness loomed an ominous shape. Just in time, the three teenagers dived behind a fallen tree, as a large adult tiger padded silently into the open and sniffed the air. Clearly, it had dinner on its mind ...

"Maybe that's what Arun was trying to tell Mya," Kate whispered to Kobe. "He was warning her about the tiger."

Kobe wasn't listening. He was too busy staring at the GPS screen. "I don't get it," he murmured. "According to this, the tiger is standing exactly where our tracker should be."

Kate gulped as the explanation dawned on her. "The tiger must have eaten the wolf ... or ... " Suddenly, she stopped short.

"Or Arun," finished Kobe, saying the words that Kate could not, but softly, so that Mya wouldn't hear. She had just found her brother and both agents knew that she would be more than heartbroken at the thought that she might have lost him again so soon.

As Kobe spoke, the red dot on the screen— and the tiger—began to move.

"It's heading toward us," he whispered. "It must have picked up our scent. We need Jack, and we need him quick! Can you radio him?"

"Already done," replied Kate. "He's on his way. But we're going to have deal with this ourselves until he gets here ..."

Mya shrieked as the tiger launched itself through the air toward the fallen tree. "LOOK OUT!"

In a split second, Kobe, Kate, and Mya leaped to one side and rolled across the forest floor—straight toward a steep ravine. As quick as a flash, Mya made a grab for Kate's arm, pulling her back from the rocky edge as she came dangerously close to it.

"MOVE! NOW!" yelled Kobe, as the tiger prepared to pounce a second time.

Mya struggled to her feet, but slipped and fell, landing with her foot caught between two rocks.

"Help me!" she cried. "I'm stuck!"

Kate and Kobe rushed to free her, but she was caught fast.

The tiger started to close in ...

"Save yourselves," cried Mya, tugging at her foot in desperation. "Just promise to find Arun for me."

Kobe shook his head. "We're not going anywhere without you. We're all in this together!" He gave Mya's foot one last pull, and it started to move in his hand. She was free at last!

The three teenagers backed up slowly, as the hungry tiger closed in on them, pinning them up against a rock. There was nowhere left to go ...

Into the Ravine

Suddenly, Arun exploded out of the bushes and sprang on the tiger's back, snarling and clawing at it like a wolf. The tiger let out an angry roar, twisting and writhing about as it tried to swat him away with an enormous paw. Arun struggled to hold on as the furious beast whirled around and around, determined to shake off this annoying creature that had landed on it. THUD! Mya, Kobe, and Kate watched in horror as Arun fell to the ground and the tiger aimed a vicious swipe at his head. But it was too slow! With lightning speed, the boy rolled over and jumped to his feet, sneering and growling. The furious tiger sprang at Arun, but this time the boy was ready. Leaping to one side,

he scrambled up onto a fallen tree, launched himself over the tiger, and landed on the edge of the ravine. Snapping and snarling, he ran back and forth, taunting the tiger, as if daring it to follow. Enraged, the tiger lunged at the boy—but Arun was too quick for it. He sprang into the undergrowth, as the tiger chased after him roaring with fury.

For a moment, all Kobe, Kate, and Mya could do was stare after them, unable to believe what they had witnessed.

>> A New Jersey cat with no claws scared a bear up a tree in its back yard in 2006, not coming down until the cat's owner called her off.

>> A dog saved its owners from a mountain lion attack in California in 2009. Hoagie, a black Labrador mix, needed five hours of surgery after the fight, but survived.

"He's alive!" Mya whispered, breaking the silence. "He came back to save us."

"He's incredible," said Kobe, his voice shaking from shock. "I can't believe he took on a tiger and won!"

"For now, maybe," said Kate. "But how long can he hold out against a creature that powerful?"

The three teenagers shivered as the full meaning of Kate's words hit them.

"Hurry!" cried Mya, pulling Kobe and Kate toward the ravine. "We've got to go help him!"

Kobe looked at the GPS system. "Let's go!" he said. "There's no time to wait for Jack. Every minute could count. At least we know which target is which now ..."

As they made their way, Kobe studied the screen carefully. The two red dots were following the edge of the ravine, just a few yards apart. It was a beautifully clear night and the moon gave a lot of light, but the shadows it cast still made moving through the unfamiliar landscape difficult.

"Watch out!" Kobe called as they stumbled over the uneven ground. "We're very close to the edge here. The ground may not be that stable."

Just as they reached a rocky outcrop, Kobe signaled for them to stop.

"Sshh!" he whispered in a low voice. "Keep absolutely still. Someone's coming."

Kate and Mya froze. The sound of branches and twigs snapping underfoot was growing louder and louder. Someone was running toward them.

Kobe made a snap decision. "Quick! Hide in here!" he said, herding the others into a small cave. "And keep out of sight."

They watched from their hiding place as a figure ran through the bushes, headed straight for the edge of the ravine, with the tiger close behind.

"Is that ... Arun?" asked Mya, her voice faint with fear.

Suddenly, the figure stumbled and fell as the ground gave way, and slid over the edge in a shower of rocks and earth. The night was filled with the sound of falling debris. With a roar of fury, the tiger watched as its prey vanished

before its eyes, down into the ravine below.

His heart pounding, Kobe checked the GPS. One red dot flashed inside the ravine, while the second—the tiger—moved back and forth along the edge. A pained howl rose up from below and echoed through the cold night air, confirming what Kobe already knew. It was Arun in the ravine—and he was trapped!

Horrified, the two agents and Mya watched helplessly as the tiger prowled back and forth along the edge, searching for a way down to its injured prey below. It was only a matter of time ...

"I can't bear this!" cried Mya, crawling out of the cave. "I've got to do something!"

Kobe grabbed her hand and pulled her back. "Mya, listen to me!" he whispered urgently. "If you really want to help your brother, don't move. We've got to stay focused—and together. If the tiger sees you now, it will turn on you for sure. How's that going to help Arun?"

"Kobe's right," said Kate. "That tiger is clever, but we've got to be even cleverer ..."

A Question of Taste

At that moment, Kate's radio headset began to crackle.

"Jack, is that you?" she whispered into her mouthpiece. "Where are you?"

"I'm here," replied a voice from out of the darkness. The agents looked up and saw the shadowy outline of their friend in the mouth of the cave.

"Get down!" hissed Kobe. "There's a tiger out

there, and he's not feeling friendly."

Jack crawled over to the others. "Give me the lowdown. What's going on?"

"It's Arun!" cried Mya, grasping hold of Jack's arm. "He's trapped in the ravine."

Kobe quickly updated him on what had happened.

"We think Arun's hurt," he explained, "and the tiger knows it. It's trying to find a way down to get at him."

"Please help him," begged Mya. "I can't lose him now."

Jack nodded, and turned to crawl out of the cave. "Stay here," he told the others firmly, "whatever happens."

A shaft of moonlight broke through the forest as Jack slowly and calmly made his approach. Sensing his presence, the tiger stopped pacing and turned to glare at Jack, its tail lashing from side to side. Showing no fear, Jack hunkered down and began to make a strange purring noise from deep within his throat. The tiger looked at Jack, hungrily. He could tell it was readying itself to pounce. But Jack continued, trying to soothe the giant cat, making sure it could hear him above the sounds of the forest. After a moment, the tiger's tail dropped, and the fury in its eyes began to dim.

Spellbound by Jack's song, the mighty beast sank to its knees and rolled onto one side. Keeping direct eye contact, Jack moved forward, and began to stroke the tiger, still purring and murmuring continually.

▶▶ To strike up rapport with their new Siberian tiger, staff at the valley zoo in Edmonton, Alberta, had to find a French-speaking keeper. The tiger, named Boris, was born at a zoo in Quebec and only obeyed commands spoken in French.

After a moment or two the tiger stood up and stretched. Looking first toward Jack, it reached out over the edge of the ravine and sniffed the air, then it turned slowly and slipped into the forest.

"It's OK," called Jack, as the mighty beast vanished into the night. "You can come out."

The others rushed over to the ravine.

"That was awesome," said Kate, hugging Jack in relief. "What did you say to it?"

Jack smiled. "Let's just say I encouraged it to think that we would all taste really bad, and that it should look elsewhere for food."

"I told you we needed to be clever!" laughed Kate.

"Hey!" grinned Jack. "Less of the 'we', if you please ..."

Kate opened her rucksack, pulled out a powerful nightlight, and shone it down into the ravine. In the gloom, they could just make out the shape of Arun, slumped against the rock face on a ledge. His leg was twisted awkwardly, and he appeared to be hurt.

"We're coming for you, Arun," called Mya,

shining the light onto the ledge. "Don't move."

"Er ... good advice, team," breathed Kobe, as a low growl sounded behind them. "I don't want to freak you out, but I think we've got company."

Very slowly, Kate and the others looked over their shoulders. They were surrounded by wolves.

"Don't panic," advised Jack, swiftly checking out the wolves' body language. "I'm pretty sure that they don't mean us any harm. I think they only want to help Arun."

"I hope you're right," murmured Kate uneasily. "I really don't fancy taking on this lot right now."

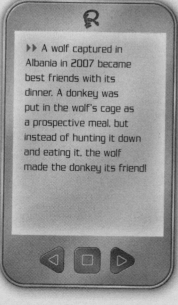

▶▶ A wolf captured in Albania in 2007 became best friends with its dinner. A donkey was put in the wolf's cage as a prospective meal, but instead of hunting it down and eating it, the wolf made the donkey its friend!

It seemed that Jack had read the situation correctly. The wolves showed no aggression toward the group. Instead, they focused all their attention on the ravine, barking and whining restlessly.

Jack opened his kit bag and removed a long rope.

"I'm going down into the ravine," he announced. "Arun will never make it out on his own. You'll have to lower me down."

Kobe looped the rope around Jack's middle and tested the knot. "That should hold."

"It better had," replied his friend. "I'm counting on it."

Very carefully, Kobe and the girls began to lower Jack down into the darkness.

"Let out a little more slack," Jack's voice called after just a few minutes. "I'm nearly there. STOP!"

As his feet hit the ledge, Jack grabbed a handhold on the side of the rock face to steady

himself. Reaching out, he offered his other hand to Arun. "Take my hand," he whispered.

Terrified and in pain, the boy stared back at Jack like a frightened rabbit. He snarled and backed up against the ledge, putting himself into a corner. Jack tried again, but Arun curled into a ball, whimpering and whining pitifully. This was going to be a lot harder than Jack had thought. Somehow, he had to calm the injured boy. He was like an animal ...

Suddenly, it hit Jack. That's exactly what Arun was—an injured animal. Kneeling down, he began to murmur softly, as if soothing a wild beast, until slowly but surely the boy began to relax. At last Arun found Jack's eyes in the darkness. Finally, reading trust in the boy's face, Jack offered out his hand once more. This time Arun took it.

Jack looped the rope around the wolf boy's waist and gave it a tug. "Pull us up," he called to the moonlit shadows standing above him. "It's time to go home ..."

The Mystery Grows

The next morning, back at the village, the agents were preparing to leave.

"Where's Jack?" asked Kate, as she checked off the final bits of Dr. Maxwell's kit. "It's nearly time to go."

"He's just recording all the vital stats for RIPLEY," said Kobe. "It certainly makes for spectacular reading. Arun is totally amazing in so many ways. He didn't just learn to communicate and behave like a wolf. His body adapted too. His muscle tone and physical abilities are quite remarkable!"

Kate nodded. "I'll never forget the sight of him leaping through the air over that tiger. It will stay with me forever."

"Me too," said Mya, coming over to join Kate and Kobe. "I'll never forget you either," she added.

Kate smiled. "Let's take a last walk together," she suggested. "We have to leave in an hour."

"I'd love to," replied Mya, taking Kate's arm. "Why don't you come with me to the temple. I want to give thanks for Arun's return."

Kate felt a strange sense of peace as they entered the cool building. There was something so calm and restful about its simplicity—rather like the village itself, really.

"It's beautiful," she told Mya, gazing around the temple with interest. "It makes me feel so peaceful."

"I used to come here every day to pray for my brother's return," Mya confided, pleased at Kate's reaction. "Now my prayers have been answered. Arun is home!"

Kate wandered over to a table in the corner, laden with carvings, photographs, jewelry, and other unusual objects.

"Those are offerings," Mya told her. "They have been left by visitors to the temple over the years."

"What's that?" asked Kate, reaching out and picking up a dusty old tin from the table. Somehow, it looked oddly familiar ... She gave it a wipe with her sleeve, and gasped. A red and yellow tin, elaborately designed, stared back at her. It was one of Ripley's clue tins. Hidden by the great man himself, these tins contained clues to the location of unique artifacts, too precious to fall into the wrong hands. But how on earth did the tin get here?

She turned to the priest, who had just come in.

"Excuse me," she asked, "but please can I take this tin? It's very important." The priest looked at her in surprise, as she searched her pockets and turned out a few English coins and a fossil she had found on her last trip with her uncle. "Can I exchange it for these?"

She smiled anxiously, but there was no need to worry. The priest nodded.

"The tin was left here many years ago by

a foreigner," he told Kate, arranging her new offerings on the table. "He said that one day someone would come back for it—and now you have."

Kate studied the tin with interest as she and Mya made their way back to the others. She was dying to open it, but wanted to wait to share her discovery with Kobe and Jack. Who was the foreigner the priest had mentioned? Could it be Robert Ripley? Maybe Kobe could throw some light on the mystery? It was part of his unique ability that he could tap into the history not only of people, but objects too. Would the tin reveal its secrets to him?

Jack and Kobe were delighted with Kate's find.

"It was just sitting there as if it was waiting for me," said Kate, when she had retold the priest's story. She handed the tin to Kobe. "Can you sense anything about its history? I think it was left here by Robert Ripley."

Kobe held the tin between his palms and closed his eyes. The image of a man—a familiar man—flashed across his mind, but Kobe couldn't quite see his face. The man was opening the tin and putting something in it. The inside of a simple church, a conversation with a priest, a table of strange objects—a series of images played in the agent's mind like a speeded-up film, until at last the man in the vision looked up, and Kobe saw his face ...

"It was Ripley," he told the others. "I'm certain of it. Everything the priest told you was true. I think we should open it."

The others agreed. With shaking hands, Kate removed the lid, pulled out a folded piece of paper, and handed it to Kobe.

"You read it," she said.

Kobe unfolded the sheet and frowned. "It's just a food order," he said, "or some kind of food delivery list, and everything is frozen on here. The date the order was placed is almost a week before the delivery date. That food must have traveled a long way. No wonder it had to be frozen, But how can this be a clue?"

He closed his eyes again for a moment as he ran his palm across the paper. "I can sense nothing from it," he told the others, a hint of frustration in his voice. "Nothing at all. But I guess I shouldn't be disappointed. It's been the same with all the clues we have found so far. This mystery just keeps growing!"

A loud beeping disturbed their thoughts.

"Sorry. That was my cell phone's alarm,"

confessed Kate. "It's time to go. Where are Mya and Arun?"

"We're here!" called Mya, leading Arun over to the group. "We wanted to say goodbye."

Mya hugged the agents one by one.

"Arun's going to live with me now," she told them. "But I know the wolves will always play an important part in his life. I can never thank you enough for what you have done. You have given me back my family."

Kate swallowed hard, fighting the tears. She knew better than anyone how precious that gift must be.

"Promise you will let us know how Arun manages," she said, taking hold of Mya's hand. "Especially with the language."

Arun's face broke into a smile.

"He knows you are talking about him," laughed Mya.

"He recognizes his name now."

"And a few other words, too," added Jack.

"Your language lessons this morning are beginning to pay off."

Right on cue, Arun spoke.

"Thank you," he said, a perfect imitation of Kate's immaculate English accent.

"That's fantastic," exclaimed Kate. "He's a natural." The three agents set off for the air strip with their guide, stopping just one last time to wave goodbye to Mya, Arun, and the villagers.

"Wait," cried Jack. "Can you hear that?" Deep in the forest, the wolves were howling.

"What do you think they are saying?" asked Kate, as they headed off.

Jack paused for a moment, then smiled. "I can't be certain, but I think they are letting Arun know how happy they are that he has found his sister."

RIPLEY'S DATABASE ENTRY

RIPLEY FILE NUMBER : 28743

MISSION BRIEF : Believe it or not sightings of a boy living with wolves have been reported. He could be a local girl's long-lost brother. Investigate accuracy of these accounts for Ripley database.

CODE NAME : Wolf Boy

REAL NAME : Arun

LOCATION : Hengduan Mountains

AGE : 13

HEIGHT : 5 ft

WEIGHT : 112 lb

VIDEO CAPTURE

UNUSUAL CHARACTERISTICS :

Long, nail-like claws, talks in barks and cries, long, tangled hair, and filthy skin.

RBI DATABASE APPROVED!

INVESTIGATING AGENTS :

Jack Stevens, Kobe Shakur, Kate Jones

▶▶ YOUR NEXT ASSIGNMENT

JOIN THE RBI IN THEIR NEXT ADVENTURE!

SECRETS OF THE DEEP

Prologue

This diving group had been really lucky. Not only had they managed to see a swordfish and a turtle, but a group of dolphins had played alongside them for almost five minutes.

As he led his group of happy tourists home, Minas noticed a large shape appear, casting a cool, gray shadow over the otherwise crystal-blue water. Minas had been a diving instructor long enough to know exactly what that particular shadow was—a very large shark.

Minas signaled that his group should follow him, hoping to move the inexperienced divers to safety before they noticed anything was wrong. But it was already too late. One by one they all saw the enormous, angry, silver shape headed toward them.

Trying his best to stay calm, Minas saw a narrow fissure in one of the rocks and guided the group inside. Outside, the shark prowled, but was too big to follow its prey in. Their hideaway led into a series of tunnels, which Minas thought could be another way out for his group. He led them as quickly and efficiently as he could through the network of darkness until suddenly the tunnel gave way to a huge cavern.

Swimming into this enormous chamber, Minas's diver's light picked out shapes and textures in the gloom that took on an eerie green glow as the shimmering yellow beam hit them. He swam further into the cave, only to quickly jump back. A gnarled hand seemed to stretch up from the ocean floor, as if reaching for him and trying to drag him down. Minas realized that the hand was not moving after all, but then saw it was not the only one. Ghostly limbs jutted out at strange angles from all over the seabed. Minas signaled for his dive group to stay where they were. This was no place for tourists. It seemed that they had stumbled on some sort of underwater graveyard, and looking at the way those bodies were reaching for help, it seemed to Minas that they were not resting peacefully.

▶▶

ENTER THE STRANGE WORLD OF RIPLEY'S...

▶▶ Believe it or not, there is a lot of truth in this remarkable tale. The Ripley's team travels the globe to track down true stories that will amaze you. Read on to find out about real Ripley's case files and discover incredible facts about some of the extraordinary people and places in our world.

Ripley's
Believe It or Not!®

▶▶ WILD CHILD

In 1992, Oxana Malaya, an eight-year-old girl was discovered in a Ukrainian village. She had been raised by a pack of wild dogs after being abandoned at the age of three.

▶▶ Oxana walked on all fours and bared her teeth.

▶▶ She would snarl, bark, and pant like a dog and had almost completely forgotten how to speak.

▶▶ Now 22, Oxana has learned to speak and act normally, but she still sleeps curled up like a dog.

credit: Discovery Channel "Wild Child" / Discovery Communications

▶▶ Found in 1954 in Lucknow, India, when he was seven years old, Ramu the wolf boy was believed to have been raised by wolves for the previous six years of his life. Stories of the found "wolf boy" reached his parents, who identified Ramu and said that he'd been snatched from his mother's lap by a wolf when he was a baby, and they believed him to be dead. Ramu made only animal noises and initially ate only raw meat and fruit.

▶▶ The Hengduan Mountains border China, Myanmar and Tibet, and rise to over 13,000 feet of incredibly tough terrain.

▶▶ The mountains are one of the few places to see the rare giant panda. There are thought to be fewer than 2000 pandas living in the wild.

▶▶ Nomadic people still roam the region, grazing yaks thousands of feet up in the mountains.

▶▶ The area is also home to the snow leopard, which is extremely rare.

▶▶ Ancient traders would carry tea across the treacherous mountains in caravans pulled by horses.

▶▶ Hengduan is so extreme that the climate can be completely different from peak to peak, from dense rainforest to snow-covered summits.

▶▶ The mountains are home to at least 3500 native species of plants.

▶▶ WOLF MAN

Over many years, Briton Shaun Ellis has learned the ways of the wolf and is welcomed into dangerous wild packs.

▶▶ Shaun has studied their body language and sounds, and knows exactly how to behave.

▶▶ He will bare his teeth and stand up to aggressive wolves in the pack, aiming to become top dog.

▶▶ Shaun has received countless bites from wolves, but he says that wolf saliva helps to heal them.

credit: Richard Austin/Rex Features

▶▶ Shaun Ellis has lived with packs of wild wolves in the Rocky Mountains, communicating with sound and scent.

credit: © Pavel Losevsky—Fotolia.com

▶▶ The wolf has extremely powerful jaws capable of generating over 400 pounds of pressure—four times as strong as human jaws, and with much sharper teeth!

▶▶ The heaviest wolf ever was discovered in Ukraine. It weighed 194 pounds, the same as two ten-year-old boys.

WILD WOLF PACKS

▶▶ Wolves have been around for 300,000 years.

▶▶ They can chase prey at 40 mph for sustained periods.

▶▶ Wolves are thought to be smarter than domestic dogs, which they outperformed in mental tests set in 2009.

▶▶ A pack of hungry wolves is capable of chasing and killing an adult moose weighing well over 1000 pounds.

▶▶ Packs communicate with body language, facial expressions, sounds, and smells.

▶▶ LION-FACED BOY

credit: Ripley Entertainment

▶▶ Although very hairy, Hypertrichosis sufferers don't usually have hair on their palms and the soles of their feet.

Known as "Lionel the Lion-faced Boy," Russian Stephen Bilgraski performed in the USA with Barnum and Bailey's circus in the mid-19th century.

▶▶ He was almost completely covered in thick hair.

▶▶ His excess hair was probably caused by Hypertrichosis, which affects only one in a billion people.

▶▶ It is a problem that can affect whole families.

►► RIPLEY

►► In his lifetime, Ripley traveled over 450,000 miles looking for oddities—the distance from Earth to the Moon and back again.

►► Ripley had a large collection of cars, but he couldn't drive. He also bought a Chinese sailing boat, called Mon Lei, but he couldn't swim.

►► Ripley was so popular that his weekly mailbag often exceeded 170,000 letters, all full of weird and wacky suggestions for his cartoon strip.

►► He kept a 20-foot-long boa constrictor as a pet in his New York home.

►► Ripley's Believe It or Not! cartoon is the longest-running cartoon strip in the world, read in 42 countries and 17 languages every day.

In 1918, Robert Ripley became fascinated by strange facts while he was working as a cartoonist at the *New York Globe*. He was passionate about travel and, by 1940, had visited no less than 201 countries, gathering artifacts and searching for stories that would be right for his column, which he named Believe It or Not!

Ripley bought an island estate at Mamaroneck, New York, and filled the huge house there with unusual objects and odd creatures that he'd collected on his explorations.